PUFFIN BOOKS

Sky Horses

The Royal Foal

The second book in the quartet

Linda Chapman lives in Leicestershire with her family and two Bernese mountain dogs. When she is not writing, she spends her time looking after her two young daughters and baby son, horse riding and talking to people about writing.

You can find out more about Linda on her websites *lindachapman.co.uk* and *lindachapman author.co.uk*

D1146542

Books by Linda Chapman

BRIGHT LIGHTS

CENTRE STAGE

MY SECRET UNICORN series

NOT QUITE A MERMAID series

SKY HORSES series

STARDUST series

UNICORN SCHOOL series

LINDA CHAPMAN

Sky Horses

The Royal Foal

Illustrated by Ann Kronheimer

PUFFIN

PUFFIN BOOKS

Published by the Penguin Group
Penguin Books Ltd, 80 Strand, London WC2R ORL, England
Penguin Group (USA) Inc., 375 Hudson Street, New York, New York 10014, USA
Penguin Group (Canada), 90 Eglinton Avenue East, Suite 700, Toronto, Ontario, Canada M4P 2Y3
(a division of Pearson Penguin Canada Inc.)
Penguin Ireland, 25 St Stephen's Green, Dublin 2, Ireland (a division of Penguin Books Ltd)
Penguin Group (Australia), 250 Camberwell Road, Camberwell, Victoria 3124, Australia
(a division of Pearson Australia Group Pty Ltd)
Penguin Books India Pvt Ltd, 11 Community Centre, Panchsheel Park, New Delhi – 110 017, India
Penguin Group (NZ), 67 Apollo Drive, Rosedale, North Shore 0632, New Zealand
(a division of Pearson New Zealand Ltd)
Penguin Books (South Africa) (Pty) Ltd, 24 Sturdee Avenue, Rosebank,
Johannesburg 2196, South Africa

Penguin Books Ltd, Registered Offices: 80 Strand, London WC2R ORL, England

puffinbooks.com

First published 2009
1

Text copyright © Linda Chapman, 2009
Illustrations copyright © Ann Kronheimer, 2009
All rights reserved

The moral right of the author and illustrator has been asserted

Set in Bembo 15/22pt
Typeset by Palimpsest Book Production Limited, Grangemouth, Stirlingshire
Made and printed in England by Clays Ltd, St Ives plc

British Library Cataloguing in Publication Data
A CIP catalogue record for this book is available from the British Library

ISBN 978-0-141-32331-2

www.greenpenguin.co.uk

Penguin Books is committed to a sustainable future
for our business, our readers and our planet.
The book in your hands is made from paper
certified by the Forest Stewardship Council.

To everyone who put up with
me while I wrote these books

Day
One

The cave was dimly lit. Candles sent shadows flickering up the damp walls and, outside, the sea crashed on the shingle beach. Heavy clouds smothered the stars in the night sky.

A woman in a silvery-blue dress was marking out a circle on the cave floor with stones. Her face was beautiful, her eyes intent on what she was doing. 'Between the sea and the sky, where no ordinary human can reach,' she said softly as she joined up the ends of the circle. Carefully, she placed four objects from a small table around it – a jar of earth, a small glass bottle with a stopper, a metal dish into which she poured some water and a lit candle that she took from one of the rocky ledges, its flame flickering weakly. 'The magic will begin.'

The woman pushed back her long dark-blonde hair and walked to the cave opening. 'Six days for a hidden stone to show itself,' she murmured, looking out at the sea.

Taking three more stones out of her pocket, she turned them over in her hands, then went back to the circle and knelt down just outside it. 'The seeing stone,' she said, placing a stone with a single hole through its centre to her left. The next stone she placed to her right. It had two holes through it. 'The warding stone,' she muttered.

Now she had just one stone left. She held it up. It was pale brown with a small hole through the centre that was blocked with a chip of stone.

Her voice hardened to ice. 'The trapping stone.'

She placed it inside the circle and clapped her hands. 'Appear, Prince!'

A thin stream of mist flooded out of

the hole in the stone. It flowed into the centre of the circle where it formed the tiny but perfect shape of a young grey horse, no bigger than the woman's hand. He looked barely older than a foal: his tail was still not full length, his mane stuck up slightly, his legs were long and gangly. He snorted – his dark eyes wide and astonished – but then, seeing the woman, his ears instantly flattened. He squealed and reared up, his front legs striking out.

She laughed. 'You cannot fight me, Prince of the Sky!'

Swinging round, the tiny horse galloped towards the circle's edge, but as he reached the wall of stones he collided with it and staggered backwards.

'There is no escape.' The woman's
blue eyes glinted as she spoke. 'You *will*
do as I say.'

The colt squealed in defiance.

The woman swept up the stone and
tightened her fingers round it. The colt
immediately crashed to his knees. She
watched him coldly as he struggled to
his feet. When he tried to plunge
forward, the woman snapped out a
word. The colt stopped mid-rear, a look

of sudden obedience coming over his
face. He dropped his front hooves to
the ground. 'Lead the sky herd,' the
woman commanded. 'Clear the skies.'

She lifted the hand that was not
holding the stone and clicked her
fingers again. A group of shadowy
horses appeared in the circle, young and
old, all shades of grey from the purest
white to the darkest steel, manes and
tails sweeping to the floor, eyes dark
and alert. They massed around the colt
as if looking to him for instruction. A
beautiful snow-white mare pushed her
way through the crowd and nuzzled his
neck anxiously. But the colt didn't seem
to see her.

He walked slowly forward, his eyes
empty and vacant. The horses in front

of him parted to let him through and then followed him.

He led them towards the far side of the circle. As he got to the edge, he stopped, but the other horses walked straight on past. Reaching the wall of stones, they each vanished. At last the only one left was the colt. He hung his head, his eyes seeming to see nothing.

The woman held out the stone, the hole pointing towards the colt. She muttered something under her breath. The colt shivered and dissolved into a stream of mist. The mist flowed back into the hole until the circle was completely empty.

The woman looked towards the cave opening. The wind had dropped and stars were now shining out, bright pinpricks of light in the velvety-black sky. Every cloud had disappeared across the horizon. A smile curved at her lips.

'And so day one begins,' she whispered.

CHAPTER
One

'Got you!'

'No! Got *you*!'

'Got you back!'

Erin and her best friend, Chloe, giggled as they flew through the night sky, playing tag.

'OK, you win.' Erin gave in. 'I'm it.' She knew Chloe would never stop until she had won. She twirled around in the sky, her blue dress glittering in

the starlight. *I love being a stardust spirit*, she thought.

A few days ago, a whole new world of magic had opened up for her when she had found out that some people could turn into stardust spirits who could fly and do magic, and she was one of them! She had also discovered that there were horses living in the clouds – and that she was actually a special kind of stardust spirit called a weather weaver, who could work with the sky horses to change the weather. Erin had always believed in magic, so finding out it was real had been brilliant, but also quite scary. She glanced at Chloe. She was very, very glad she had a best friend to share it with.

Chloe looked back at her and grinned. 'It's so weird to think that a week ago we had no idea we were stardust spirits, isn't it? That we didn't even know each other, and now we're best friends!'

Erin felt a warm glow. She loved the fact that she and Chloe often seemed to be thinking the same thing. 'I wonder what we would have said if someone had told us about it all.'

'*Cool!*' said Chloe with a grin. 'That's what I would have said, I mean. Wouldn't you?'

Erin hesitated. Lots of it *was* cool – doing magic, being best friends with Chloe – but there was other stuff that was less good. The night before they'd had to fight a dark stardust spirit called Marianne and that had been very scary. Marianne had captured the leader of the sky horses, a beautiful stallion called Tor. She had brought him to Earth, and had been trying to use him to control the weather. Erin and Chloe had freed him, but, just as he had been about to fly back home through a giant stone gateway that bridged the cloud world and Earth, his son, a young colt, jumped through it.

Marianne had immediately captured the colt, turning him into mist and sucking him into a type of hagstone that Tor had later explained to them was called a trapping stone.

Erin and Chloe had promised Tor that they would do everything they could to help him free his son, Mistral. In fact, they were now on their way to meet Tor so that they could start planning how they would rescue the colt.

'I wonder where Marianne is right now,' said Erin uneasily. 'And what she's doing with Mistral.'

Erin had so many questions. The last few days had been taken up with trying to rescue Tor and she had learnt very little about how weather weavers worked their magic and what it really meant to be one. All she knew was that weather weavers used hagstones, stones with holes in that could be found on the beach or by water. There were different types of hagstones, some with one hole, some with more, and they each contained a different type of magic that a weather weaver could free and use. 'Let's ask Tor,' she said.

They sped on over the cliff top. To their left the sea broke against the beach, the waves raking at the shingle. Behind them the lights in the village of Long Medlow twinkled in the dark. They reached a wood and flew down.

With a low whinny, a magnificent grey stallion stepped out of the shadows into a clearing below, his mane and tail sweeping to the floor, his ears pricked.

'Tor!' Erin greeted him in delight.

Tor could appear either in a cloud form, where he looked as if he was made of mist, or as a real, solid horse. For now, he had chosen his solid form. His hooves sank slightly into the soft ground and there were flecks of mud around his fetlocks.

Erin landed on the grass in front of him. He whickered softly and touched his nose to her shoulder, his breath whispering across the bare skin of her arms.

She wanted to put her arms round him, but didn't quite dare. He nuzzled her and she smiled up at him. He was huge, about seventeen hands high.

'Hi, Tor,' said Chloe, landing beside Erin.

Tor reached out and touched her arm too. 'I am glad you have come, girls. We must act quickly and find the trapping stone so that we can free Mistral. Marianne could use him to bring great storms, tornadoes, hurricanes . . .'

'How will she do that? I mean how *do* the sky horses control the weather?' asked Erin. There was so much she still didn't understand about weather weaving.

'We do not control the weather, Erin,' Tor explained gently. 'We *are* the weather. The skies change with our many moods and movements. If we are quiet and peaceful, the clouds float gently. If we move swiftly, the clouds race across the sky. If we mass together, the clouds grow darker and heavier with rain. If we cross over the horizon, then the skies clear of all clouds. The leader of the herd decides what will happen, and as the herd follows him the weather changes.'

'What I don't get is why Marianne needed to capture you and Mistral,' said Chloe. 'If she's a weather weaver, can't she make the sky horses change the weather anyway?'

Tor shook his head. 'No one can make the sky horses change the weather. A weather weaver may talk to the sky horses using hagstones. They can ask the horses to change the weather, but the lead stallion will always make the final decision. A weather weaver only has real control over the weather if they have a sky horse of royal blood in their power here on Earth. Now Marianne has

Mistral under her control, she will use a hagstone to send an image of him into the skies. He will appear there in a misty form. She will tell him what to do, the other horses will follow his lead and so the weather will come under her command.'

'But why does she want to do that?' Erin asked.

'For power,' Tor replied abruptly. 'If she has complete control over the weather, she will be able to wreak havoc over the coast and make all people fear her. Many years ago another dark spirit captured my grandfather, who was king of the sky horses then. There were great storms until that spirit was defeated.' He looked seriously at them both. 'Now the three of us must defeat Marianne.'

'We will!' declared Chloe.

Erin nodded. 'We'll find the trapping stone and set Mistral free.'

'Unfortunately, before we manage to do that, Marianne might cause great storms to come,' said Tor. 'I will need you to use your weather-weaving magic, Erin, to cast visions of me into

the clouds just as Marianne will do with Mistral. I will try to change what she is doing, calming my herd, stopping the storms.'

'But won't Marianne try to stop you?' Chloe burst out.

Tor nodded. 'Yes, it will be dangerous – for all of us.'

'I don't care,' interrupted Erin, doing her best to sound brave although her heart was pounding. 'I'll do whatever you say. We can't let Marianne start massive storms and put everyone in danger here.'

Tor nuzzled her gratefully. 'You are very courageous.'

'We'd better find the trapping stone as quickly as we can so we can free Mistral,' said Chloe. 'I wonder where Marianne is keeping it?'

'I believe she will be hiding it outdoors in a place where she can work her magic,' said Tor. 'But there is no need for you to follow her. Erin can use her weather-weaving powers to discover the stone's hiding place.'

'How?' asked Erin.

'Bring a seeing stone and also a warding stone, a hagstone with two holes, tomorrow night, and then I will teach you how to use them both to do this safely.' Tor's voice took on a warning note. 'But do not attempt to see Marianne on your own. It could be very risky.'

'I won't,' Erin promised.

'Good,' Tor answered. 'And in the meantime be on the lookout for danger. There is always the possibility that

Marianne may come looking for you. Take a hair from my mane. If you need to reach me for whatever reason, hold the hair and call to me. Wherever you are, the cloud magic that runs through me means I will hear and reply.'

Erin looked at his long mane and hesitated. She felt shy about breaking even a strand. 'Do I really need to?' she asked. 'Can't I use a hagstone? You've talked to me that way before, Tor.' She had first heard Tor's voice speaking to her when she had been holding a hagstone in her bedroom.

'I can talk to you when you are holding a hagstone and one day you too will learn to be able to contact me in the same way, but at the moment you do not have the knowledge and control to accurately use a hagstone to contact me,' the stallion replied. 'If you have a hair of my mane, you will be able to speak to me easily at any time if you need to. It will be safer this way. The magic is stronger and simpler.' He nudged her with his muzzle. 'Go on.'

Erin cautiously broke off a single hair.

Tor's dark eyes met hers. 'Use it whenever you need to.'

Holding the hair tight, Erin rose into the air. Chloe followed her. As they reached the treetops, Erin glanced down. Tor had melted away into the woods and the glade was empty.

Chloe looked at her almost enviously. 'I wish I was a weather weaver and could do magic like you.'

Erin felt a bit daunted. 'I hope I *can* do the magic Tor needs me to.'

'Of course you can!' Chloe squeezed her hand.

Erin felt lifted by Chloe's confidence. *Chloe's right*, she thought. *I'm going to help Tor. We're going to find the trapping stone and set Mistral free!*

CHAPTER
Two

As they left the woods, they flew over three ponies in a cliff-top field. 'Let's go and see them!' Chloe called to Erin.

They swooped down and landed on the grass. One of the ponies was lying down; the other two were dozing standing up, hind legs resting. They lifted their heads, pricking their ears as they saw Erin and Chloe. Animals were never scared of stardust spirits. One of the ponies, a chestnut, whickered at them.

Erin and Chloe went over. While
Chloe cuddled the two who were
standing up, Erin crouched down beside
the piebald pony on the ground. He
nuzzled her hands.

'Hey, boy,' she said, stroking his nose.

'I wonder who we'll get to ride
tomorrow at the stables,' said Chloe. She
and Erin went to the same riding
stables. They helped there at the
weekends and in the holidays in
exchange for rides and free lessons. She
grinned at Erin. 'Let me guess: I bet
you'll be wanting Kestrel.'

Kestrel was a new pony at the stables.
He had just arrived the day before. He
was a young dapple-grey, part Arab
pony, and Erin thought he was
gorgeous.

'I hope I get him,' said Erin eagerly.
'But then everyone wants to ride
him.'

'Well, I don't really mind if I do or
not,' said Chloe generously. 'If I get
given him for the lesson, we can ask
Jackie if we can swap.'

Erin smiled at her. 'Thanks!' She
sighed longingly. 'I really wish I had a
pony of my own.'

'Me too,' said Chloe. 'Still, at least

we've got the ponies at the stables to look after.' She gave the chestnut a last pat. 'Why don't we practise using our stardust powers now? I want to do some summer magic!'

Erin nodded. 'OK. But we'd better go somewhere more hidden than this.'

They left the ponies and found a quiet, secluded place on the cliff top. There were four different types of stardust spirit – summer, autumn, winter and spring – and they could each do a different kind of magic. Chloe was a summer spirit, which meant she could start fires. Like all weather weavers, Erin was a winter spirit, which meant she could make it rain, snow or hail. She hadn't been very good at doing her winter magic at first. Her rainclouds kept soaking her, and when she tried to get hail she got snow, and when she tried to get snow she got rain, but the night before when they had been fighting Marianne she had managed to conjure up a raincloud just when she needed it.

As she and Chloe practised, she made it rain in different places and began practising how to move rainclouds around and make the rain heavier or lighter.

'That's really good,' said Chloe, looking impressed as Erin made a raincloud change from drizzling to pouring and then back to drizzling.

'Thanks.' Erin smiled. 'It feels much easier tonight.'

'I bet that's because you believe you'll

be able to do it now,' said Chloe. 'Xanthe always says that's the most important thing with magic.'

Xanthe was Chloe's godmother. She was an adult stardust spirit and she had helped them the night before when they had set Tor free. Unfortunately she didn't live close by. That morning she'd had to return to Devon where she lived with her daughter, Allegra, but she had promised to come back again as soon as she could.

Chloe put out a fire she had made with a wave of her hand. 'Let's have a race!'

Erin laughed, glad to have a chance to play. She flew after Chloe and together they swooped through the sky.

★

When Erin woke up the next morning, the sun was shining through her window and the house was already alive with its usual noise. The TV in the lounge was showing a football programme and from the kitchen there was the sound of a sports station playing on the radio. Jake, her twelve-year-old stepbrother, was shouting down the stairs to her dad about a tennis tournament he was playing in that day.

Rubbing her eyes, she got up. Sam and Ben, her other two stepbrothers, were in the kitchen. They were eating huge bowls of cereal and talking about windsurfing.

'Pity there's no wind today,' Ben commented, looking out of the window.

'We won't have a chance to get up on the boards.'

The sky was a perfect blue without a single cloud in sight. Erin felt a wave of relief as she looked at it. It looked like Marianne hadn't started trying to use Mistral to cause chaos with the weather yet. That seemed a bit strange. Only a few days ago massive storms had been threatening. Why *was* everything so calm? She shrugged to herself, deciding to just feel glad that it was.

'You going horse riding today, squirt?' Sam asked her.

'Yep,' she said, getting a muffin out of the bread bin.

There was the sound of feet thundering on the stairs and Jake burst into the kitchen. He had a tennis ball in his hand. He chucked it at Ben, who caught it easily and chucked it back, making Erin duck as it almost hit her head. Jake grabbed it and, pushing past Erin, swiped the muffin.

'Hey! I was going to have that!' she protested.

'And now you're not!' Jake grinned, taking a huge bite. He picked up a carton of orange juice from the table

and drank it straight from the spout.

'Jake! You know Jo hates you doing that!' Erin exclaimed.

'Who's going to tell her?' Jake challenged.

'Tell me what?' Jo, Erin's stepmum, came into the kitchen.

'Nothing, Mum,' Jake said with a grin, hastily putting the carton down.

Jo looked at Erin. 'Nothing,' Erin agreed. Her stepbrothers could be really annoying — especially Jake — but most of the time she got on OK with them and she didn't want to get them into trouble.

Jo went over to the kettle. 'What are you doing at the stables today?' she asked Erin.

'Well, there's a new pony,' said Erin, trying to turn her thoughts to normal things and away from magic. 'He's called Kestrel and he's gorgeous. He arrived yesterday. I really want to ride him. No one's ridden him in a lesson yet, but Jackie said one of us could try him out today. I really hope I get to . . .'

Erin's voice was drowned out as behind her Sam and Ben started arguing about whether they would go swimming or play cricket seeing as they couldn't windsurf, and Jake turned the radio up.

'I'll give you a lift to the stables in half an hour,' Jo said, above the noise.

Erin nodded and thankfully left the noisy kitchen to go and get dressed.

When Erin got to Hawthorn Stables, she headed to the tack room to put away her lunchbox. Fran and Katie, two of the other helpers and Erin's ex-best friends, were in there. They glanced up as she came in.

'Hi,' muttered Erin.

'Hi,' said Katie briefly.

Fran didn't say anything. She had short blonde hair and big blue eyes. Katie was much taller with brown hair tied back in a ponytail. They went to the same school as Erin and she used to be friends with them, but a few months ago they had found out that she was going to go to a different secondary school from them in September and since then they had been leaving her out and being mean to her.

Erin tried to pretend she didn't care, but she did. She'd been very glad when she had met Chloe a week ago and become best friends with her. They didn't go to the same school at the moment, but at least they went riding together now and could meet at night time as stardust spirits.

Now she had to step over Fran and Katie's legs to put her lunchbox away, and, although Katie shifted her feet out of the way slightly, Fran didn't budge. She just stared at her, almost as if she was daring Erin to ask her to move. Erin could feel herself blushing.

She put her lunchbox down and Fran lifted her leg. She smirked as Erin stumbled against one of the saddles.

'I wonder who we'll get to ride in the lesson today,' said Katie.

'I really want to ride Kestrel,' replied Fran. 'Jackie says he's brilliant at jumping.' She looked at Erin. 'Bet you won't get to ride him ever. Jackie usually gives you all the ancient ponies, like old Wilf.' She grinned. Wilf was the oldest and slowest pony at the stables.

Erin heard Chloe calling her outside. She went out to meet her.

'Hiya!' said Chloe.

Jackie looked out of the office. 'Hey, you two, could you bring in Pippin and Kestrel for me, please? They're in the top field.'

'Sure,' Chloe replied. 'Who are we going to ride today, Jackie?'

'You'll be on Smoky, Chloe, and I thought you could ride Kestrel today, Erin.'

Erin felt a rush of delight. So she was

going to ride him after all! Chloe grinned at her.

When they reached the field, Erin called Kestrel's name. He lifted his head and walked over with his ears pricked. He was a beautiful pony with a dished face, large dark eyes and a long silky forelock. Erin clipped on his lead rope and he pushed his nose affectionately against her shoulder.

Chloe joined her with Pippin, and they led the two ponies back to the yard. When they got there, Fran and Katie came over. Fran gave Erin a sour look. 'Jackie says *you're* riding Kestrel. Well, I bet you won't be able to cope with him. Jackie told me he's really lively.'

Erin blushed and turned to go, but Chloe had overheard. 'Of course Erin

will be able to cope,' she said loyally.
'She's a much better rider than you,
Fran!'

'Let's go, Chloe,' said Erin, tugging
Chloe's arm. She hated arguments.
Chloe frowned and for a moment Erin
thought she was going to argue further,
but then she gave in and they led the
ponies away.

'I don't know why you don't stand up to those two more,' said Chloe. 'You should just tell them to get lost when they're mean to you.'

Erin wished she could, but she always worried that if she said anything back then Fran and Katie would be even nastier. It was easier just to keep quiet. However, she knew Chloe wouldn't understand that. Chloe was so brave and never frightened of anyone or anything.

'Just forget it,' she sighed. 'Let's get grooming.'

An hour later, Erin was riding proudly round the ring on Kestrel. At first he was very well behaved, but as they started to trot he began to shake his head and try to catch up with Misty in front of him. Erin struggled to slow him down.

'Steady, boy,' she whispered. But he didn't listen; he pulled at the reins and went faster, almost bumping into Misty. She put her ears back and squealed, and Katie, who was riding her, gave Erin a cross look.

Erin circled Kestrel into a space. He almost bounded into a canter. She pulled on the reins.

'Are you OK, Erin?' asked Jackie.

'Yes, fine!' gasped Erin, going red as everyone looked at her.

To her relief, Jackie told them all to walk again and Erin began to get Kestrel more under control, but then Jackie told them to trot.

Kestrel speeded up. Erin's throat

tightened. She closed her fingers on the reins. He threw his head up and down, making her wobble in the saddle.

'Keep him steady, Erin,' warned Jackie.

Kestrel shied. Erin lost a stirrup and grabbed at his mane. Feeling her hold loosen on the reins, Kestrel plunged forward. Erin tried to stop him, but he wouldn't listen. He set off round the ring at a canter.

'Whoa!' Erin gasped, pulling on the reins, but he was too strong. She couldn't stop him!

'Sit down in the saddle, Erin!' Jackie shouted. 'Turn him in a circle!'

Erin's heart pounded as Kestrel raced past the other ponies and veered round the corner. His legs slipped and she thought he was going to fall over. She pulled as hard as she could on the left rein. He started to turn. She kept pulling and as he circled he began to slow down. With a snort, he dropped back to a trot. Feeling sick, Erin halted him.

Jackie strode over. 'Are you OK?'

Erin nodded, trying to blink back the tears that were prickling her eyes. She caught Chloe's sympathetic look.

'I said he was too lively for you to ride,' Katie muttered from Misty's back.

Jackie didn't hear. 'You did very well to stop him, Erin,' she said. 'I never expected him to be so lively. I should have lunged him before the lesson. Look, why don't you take him in and tack Wilf up?'

Erin slid off his back. Her legs were trembling so much that as her feet met the ground she almost fell over. She caught Kestrel's saddle to steady herself and Fran sniggered.

'Take him in and come back as quickly as you can,' Jackie told her.

Erin put Kestrel in his stable and, after giving him a quick, nervous look, she tacked Wilf up. She rode into the school and joined in behind Katie. Katie looked round and smirked at her. Erin felt her cheeks burn and looked away. She caught sight of a long grey hair from Kestrel's mane caught on the back of her glove, and an image of Tor telling her to take a hair from his mane the night before flashed quickly into her mind. She felt a little better as she imagined what Fran and Katie would say if they knew she was a stardust spirit with special powers who was friends with a sky stallion.

Oh, she thought. *If only they knew.*

CHAPTER

Three

'How was your day at the stables?' asked
Jo when she collected Erin that
afternoon. 'Did you have a good lesson?'

'Mmm.' Erin didn't want to talk
about Kestrel cantering off with her, so
she changed the subject. 'What have
you been doing?'

'I went out for a bike ride with your
dad this morning,' Jo replied. 'Then I
went round to see Aunt Alice. She's
going to have supper with us tonight. I

thought we could pick her up in the car now to save her walking to ours.'

Aunt Alice was Jo's great-aunt. She was very old and she moved very stiffly now, but she still lived in her own cottage and her mind was very sharp. Erin often went to visit her with Jo, and Aunt Alice would tell her all sorts of amazing stories about the past.

They drew up outside the house. Erin jumped out of the car. 'Hi!' she said, as Aunt Alice opened the cottage door.

'Hello, dear,' said Aunt Alice. 'How were the horses today?'

'Oh, fine,' said Erin quickly.

'I remember when I was eleven,' said Aunt Alice, getting her coat. 'My friend Dolly lived on a farm and she had three ponies . . .'

'Solo, Finch and Beauty,' Erin said, following her. She'd heard about the ponies Aunt Alice used to ride many times before.

Aunt Alice smiled. 'That's right. We used to take them on to the beach. One day we rode out to Four Rocks, but the tide came in and cut us off. We had to swim back to the beach on the ponies.'

Erin had heard this story too. 'I thought that happened when you had a picnic by the rocks at World's End?' she said.

'Four Rocks is just another name for World's End, dear,' said Aunt Alice.

'But why was it called Four Rocks?' asked Erin, thinking about World's End where there were two straight stones that jutted into the sky and one giant hagstone with a hole big enough for an adult to climb through. They were on a spit of land not far from where Aunt Alice lived. 'There are only three rocks.'

Aunt Alice looked puzzled. 'You know, I can't remember why it was called Four Rocks. But I always liked going there.'

Erin wondered what Aunt Alice would say if she knew that the giant round stone was the gateway between their world and

the world of the sky horses. It was there that Marianne had captured Mistral.

'Anyway, enough of my old memories,' said Aunt Alice with a smile. 'Let's get into the car and you can tell me all about what you've been doing today.'

Erin nodded. *Apart from Kestrel*, she added in her head.

As Erin got ready for bed that night, she found the hair from Tor's mane and wound it round the strap of her watch. It would be easier to carry around that way, and she wanted to keep it with her in case she needed to talk to him. Then she went to the window in her room where there was a small dark wooden

box. It had belonged to her real mum
and was full of hagstones. Erin's dad had
given it to Erin almost eight years ago
when her mum had died. Erin had
always liked it, but now she knew how
special it was. The ability to be a weather
weaver passed down from mother to
daughter, which meant her mum would
have been a weather weaver too. It was a
very weird thought.

There was a piece of paper near the
top of the box. Erin took it out. It had
five lines written on it:

*When the dark one returns, the door shall
be reopened
And danger will threaten all living below.
If the binding is broken, they can be
protected,*

*But one coming willingly lets the dark's
power grow
Until . . .*

Erin had always wondered what the
lines meant. The night before last,
Xanthe had said she thought they were
the start of a weather-weaving prophecy
– a prophecy that now seemed to be
coming true. Marianne was the dark
spirit whose power was growing, and
Mistral was the one who had come
through willingly.

It looked as if someone had spilt a
drink on the paper as some of the
words were washed away. Erin wondered
what else the prophecy had said.

Idly thinking about it, and worrying
about how she was going to do

weather-weaving magic that night, she
let her fingers run through the stones
and took a white one out of the box. It
was one of her mum's. Erin knew
because her mum's stones somehow felt
different from the stones she had
collected herself. They seemed to almost
buzz with energy when she held them.
The single hole in the centre was a

dark shadow. As she stared at the hole, the edges of the room around her seemed to go hazy.

For a moment the thought flashed across her mind that she should put the stone down, but the hole in the centre of the stone seemed to pull at her eyes. The smooth surface tingled beneath her fingers.

Excitement filled her. Maybe she could work out where Marianne was on her own.

How cool would that be? She imagined how pleased Tor would be, and almost before she realized what she was doing she instinctively whispered a name: 'Marianne'.

The darkness seemed to explode and suddenly she wasn't looking at a shadowy hole but at a picture – a moving image. It looked like the inside of a cave. There were rocky walls and an opening through which Erin could see the sea. Although part of her knew she was still in her bedroom, she could hear the sound of the waves crashing on the rocks,

hear the faint cry of a lone gull in the sky, smell the seaweed in the air. There was a white circle on the floor of the cave and a woman kneeling outside it. Her long blonde hair snaked down the back of her silvery-blue dress.

Marianne! The thought leapt into Erin's head.

The woman turned and her eyes seemed to look straight at Erin. She had a hagstone in her hand. 'Come!' she said quietly.

Erin hesitated. She knew that it was a bad idea, but the vision seemed to be pulling her in. *No*, she thought, trying to fight the urge.

Marianne's blue eyes met hers. 'Erin, come here.'

Her voice was soft; her smile looked reassuringly familiar. Erin's resistance melted and she stepped forward into the vision . . .

CHAPTER

Four

Erin's world turned black. For a
moment, she felt herself falling and then
she landed in a heap on the ground,
with damp rock beneath her hands. She
blinked and glanced around. She was in
a cave. There was only a split second to
take in the sound of waves crashing on
the rocks outside before Marianne
stepped in front of her. The softness had
vanished from her face.

Panic gripped Erin. She scrambled to

her feet, aware of the cold air on her bare skin.

'Bind her!' The word hissed out of the dark spirit's mouth.

Erin found she couldn't move. It was as if a giant iron fist was holding her fast. Marianne muttered a string of words. Out of nowhere, white strands of mist appeared. They wound around Erin like a cobweb. As her hands were pinned against her body, Marianne walked over and plucked the seeing stone that Erin was still clutching out of her hand.

'I have been waiting for you, Erin. I thought you would try to find me. Your powers are strong even if you do not yet know how to use them.' She regarded Erin coolly. 'What shall I do with you now?'

Erin tried to struggle, but the misty cobwebs held her fast.

Marianne laughed at her attempts to break free. 'I could take your stardust or I could just keep you here. Your body would be found in your bedroom on the floor, living and breathing – but it would seem as if you'd left it. Your mind would be gone.'

'No! Don't do that! Please!' gasped Erin, imagining how her dad and Jo would feel if they found her like that.

'Maybe not,' mused Marianne. 'I think you will be of more use to me living your usual life, but under my control. I will be able to see what the stallion is up to. A binding bracelet would mean that you'd have to do everything I said.'

'Like the binding rope you put round Tor's neck to control him?' asked Erin, a stab of fear going through her as she remembered the black rope Marianne had used to control Tor when she had first captured him. It had left raw blisters on Tor's skin and had only been broken with very difficult and dangerous magic.

'Yes.' Marianne's eyes glinted. 'But there would be no one to help you, no one to set you free. Only a weather weaver can perform the magic needed to break a binding rope. You would be under my control for as long as I wanted.'

'I'd fight you!' said Erin desperately. 'I'd fight you like Tor did.'

'He is a sky stallion; you are just a child. You wouldn't stand a chance. You would be as powerless as the foal is against me.' Moving swiftly to the back of the cave, Marianne picked a small box off a rocky ledge and, opening it, she took out a thin piece of black cord.

She turned and faced Erin.

Erin's throat went dry; her skin prickled with fear. 'No!' She struggled and screwed up her fists as she tried to push her arms away from her sides.

Marianne smiled and started walking towards her.

Suddenly, Erin felt something tickling her wrist and fingertips. She realized that it was the hair from Tor's mane. It was working itself loose from her watchstrap.

Use this hair to contact me if you need to. Tor's voice seemed to ring in her ears.

Erin clasped the hair between her fingers and pulled.

The hair tightened and for an awful moment she thought it was going to break, but then it came free.

Marianne had almost reached her. She couldn't see Erin's hands, nor what Erin was doing.

Tor! Tor! Erin yelled in her mind. *Marianne's caught me! Help me!*

She didn't know how to make the hair work or how the sky stallion could help her. Instinctively her thumb started pushing the end of the hair round to meet the hair caught between her fingers. Just as Marianne reached for her wrist, the two ends of the hair met, forming a complete circle.

There was a blinding flash of white light and Erin automatically shut her eyes. A screaming whinny filled her ears and she heard Marianne cry out in fear. Erin's eyes blinked open. 'Tor!' she gasped.

Standing just in front of her was the sky stallion. His eyes were furious. Half rearing, he plunged at the dark spirit.

'No!' Marianne stumbled back. Her foot caught on a rock and she staggered and fell, dropping the black cord and Erin's seeing stone. As it cracked to the floor, Erin felt the cobwebs start to loosen. She fought against them, tearing her hands and arms out of the white filmy strands.

Marianne's hand shot up and she pointed at Tor.

'The seeing stone, Erin!' he said, half rearing again.

Erin ripped the cobwebs off her legs and threw herself towards the hagstone. She didn't know what she had to do with it, but as her fingers closed round it she felt it tingle with magic.

Take hold of my mane! Tor's voice rang in her head. *And look into the stone.*

Clutching it tightly, Erin grabbed
Tor's mane and stared into the hagstone.

'Say where you want to go!' he
urged.

'You will not escape!' Marianne
hissed. 'Bind –'

'Home!' Erin gasped. She felt Tor
jump forward. For a moment, his mane
seemed to swirl around her like thick
icy mist. She had the sensation of
falling through whiteness and then she
landed with a bump. She stared around,

startled. She was back in her bedroom, on her own, lying on the carpet. Her eyes darted to the seeing stone in her hand. The shadowy hole was dark and seemed to draw her back to the cave. She threw it away from her. It banged into the skirting board and fell to the floor. Erin stared at it as it rocked slightly.

For a moment there was silence and then there was the sound of Jo's voice outside on the landing. 'Are you OK, Erin?'

Erin swallowed and forced her voice to sound normal. 'Yes, I'm fine. I just dropped something.'

She heard Jo's footsteps continue along the landing and down the stairs. Taking a deep, trembling breath, Erin got to her feet. Her legs felt shaky and she went to the bed. Images of the cave – of everything that had just happened – flooded in front of her eyes.

It was all too much and she covered her face with her hands. She wished she could shut out the memories, but they were vivid. Tor had said not to use a hagstone until she was with him. She should have listened. But she hadn't and Marianne had almost managed to catch her. But then Tor had come . . .

Tor! Erin felt a lurch of fear. Where was he? What had happened to him? *I hope he's OK*, she thought desperately. She looked down at her pyjamas. A long white horse hair was caught on her clothes. She seized it.

Tor, she thought. *Tor, where are you?*

In the woods. I am all right, the stallion's voice echoed in her head. *I helped you in my cloud form. Come as soon as you can safely turn into a stardust spirit.*

I will, Erin thought back. *And, Tor, I'm sorry. I know I shouldn't have looked in the stone. I shouldn't have —*

Just come. The stallion's voice broke sharply across her thoughts, cutting her off.

Erin swallowed and put the hair down. He didn't sound happy with her at all.

CHAPTER
Five

Erin lay awake, wondering what time her dad and Jo would go to bed that night. She felt sick and worried. What would Tor say to her? He'd told her not to try to see Marianne. She hadn't listened and had got into real trouble.

Don't go to bed, don't go to bed, she whispered in her head as she heard her dad pottering about. But soon she heard him go into the bedroom with Jo, and a little while later there was a faint click as the light was turned off.

Erin waited until there was absolute quiet from their room and then turned herself into a stardust spirit. Still feeling sick with nerves, she took two stones out of the box and flew to meet Chloe.

Chloe was waiting on the beach as usual. She was looking excited. 'Erin! I thought you were never going to get here! Come on! I want to get to Tor and see if he can show you how to use hagstones to spy on Marianne.'

'It's too late,' Erin told her.

Chloe frowned and Erin explained what had happened earlier.

For once, Chloe looked almost lost for words. 'Oh . . . oh, gosh.'

Erin bit her lip. 'I wonder what Tor's going to say.'

'I guess we'd better find out,' said Chloe. She squeezed Erin's hand. 'I bet he'll be OK about it,' she said, her hazel eyes hopeful. 'You were only trying to help.'

They flew to the woods together.

Tor was waiting in the clearing. He stepped forward anxiously as they came down. 'What did you do?' he said to Erin. 'What happened? How did you end up with the dark spirit?'

Erin looked at the grassy ground of the clearing. 'I was looking into a seeing stone,' she replied in a small voice. 'I felt magic happening. I said Marianne's name.'

'But I said you must not use a seeing

stone to seek her without me being there to guide you!' exclaimed Tor.

'I-I know. I'm s-sorry,' stammered Erin. 'She told me to come and I . . . I couldn't stop myself.'

'Erin was only trying to help,' Chloe put in loyally.

'But in doing so she risked everything!' Tor looked stormily at Erin. 'By

looking at a vision of Marianne, you
opened a gateway between where you
were and where she was. You let her
tempt your mind through that gateway.
You could have been trapped there,
your mind in one place, your body in
another!'

'I'm sorry!' Erin glanced at the
stallion. His body was tense. He
caught sight of her looking at him
and sighed.

'You did not fully realize the danger,'
he said more quietly. 'I did not make it
clear enough. A dark spirit like Marianne
is powerful enough to sense any
unprotected weather-weaving magic used
to spy on her. I was going to teach you
how to use a warding stone tonight so
that you could prevent Marianne from

sensing you through the seeing stone –
and harming you, Erin.'

'Oh.' Erin felt really stupid. She
remembered the vision and shuddered.
'She was going to put a binding
bracelet on me, Tor. She was going to
try to control me, but then you came.'
She looked at him. 'How?'

'You made a gateway for me with
the hair from my mane,' Tor explained.
'Hair, like stone and water, is very
powerful in weather-weaving magic. It
let me travel to you in the vision.'

'If you hadn't come . . .' Erin's voice
trailed off.

Tor nuzzled her arm and spoke softly.
'The most important thing is that you
escaped unharmed.'

Erin was eager to make amends. 'Can

you teach me how to use the stones properly now, and I'll try to see where Marianne is?'

But Tor was already shaking his head. 'We cannot use a seeing stone to watch Marianne now. Once someone has willingly entered a weather weaver's vision, the weather weaver will always have power to draw them into another vision if the gateway between them is reopened in the same way using a seeing stone.'

'Even if they're using a warding stone as well?' asked Erin, her heart sinking.

'Even then.'

Erin felt awful. 'But, if we can't use the stones to spy on her, how are we going to find out where she is keeping the trapping stone?'

There was a silence.

'Oh, Tor, I-I'm so, so sorry,' Erin stammered as she suddenly realized fully what she had done. 'I really am.'

'It cannot be helped,' the stallion sighed. 'Did Marianne give you any clues as to where the stone was?'

'No.' Erin thought back over everything that she had seen. 'I suppose it might be in the cave, but I didn't see the trapping stone and I don't know where the cave was anyway.' She felt awful. 'I've messed everything up.'

Chloe took her hand. 'You haven't. We might not be able to use a seeing stone to spy on Marianne, but we'll think of another way to find out where she is keeping the trapping stone. We can follow her or something.'

'No. That would be very dangerous.' Tor looked at Erin. 'I do not know how we will find the stone now, but you must learn to use your magic properly to protect yourself from things like this and to cast and control visions yourself.'

'Will you start teaching me?' Erin asked him. 'Now?'

'I do not think it would be wise this evening,' the stallion replied. 'You need to be calm and focused to use hagstones and you are shaken after such a fright. Bring the stones again tomorrow. We will try then. Do no use the stones before.'

He looked stern.

Erin hung her head. 'I won't. Bye, Tor,' she muttered. She followed Chloe into the sky.

Chloe shot her a sympathetic look.
'Let's do something fun!' She swooped
down and tagged Erin's arm. 'You're it!'

Erin didn't really feel like playing tag
right then, but she knew Chloe was
making an effort to make her feel
better. She flew after her and lunged for
Chloe's foot.

Chloe raced away to the left. 'Missed
me!'

Pushing the events of the evening deep down in her mind, Erin pursued her and with a surge of speed managed to touch Chloe's back. 'Got you!'

Chloe swung round and chased Erin up towards the stars.

Erin gasped, 'Rain be with me!' A raincloud appeared and rain poured down, making Chloe squeal and stop.

'Rain be gone!' said Erin hastily before her friend got too wet.

'Not fair!' exclaimed Chloe as she shook the water drops out of her eyes. 'I can't use my stardust powers to stop you tagging me. It would be much too dangerous if I was to throw a fireball at you.'

'Sorry,' said Erin. She sighed. 'I sometimes wish I could just be a normal stardust spirit – just doing this type of magic and not fighting Marianne every day. You could do that if you wanted, Chloe.'

'It wouldn't be so exciting,' said Chloe. 'I know it must have been horrid going into the vision with Marianne, but it'll be better tomorrow night when you've got Tor to help you learn to use hagstones properly. I can't believe I'm not going to be here to watch but I'm going to be staying with Xanthe and Allegra.'

With everything that had gone wrong that night with her weather-weaving magic, Erin wished Xanthe and Allegra were coming to visit Chloe, not the other way round.

Erin thought about the next night

when she would be trying to learn how to use her weather-weaving powers. Immediately she remembered Marianne walking towards her in the cave, eyes gleaming icily, and she shuddered. She wasn't going to be trying to spy on Marianne using seeing stones – she was going to be looking at other people – but what if she got it wrong? What if she made a mistake and somehow ended up using a seeing stone to look at Marianne and was pulled into her vision again?

She shivered. She wasn't looking forward to the next night at all.

CHAPTER
Six

When Erin arrived at the stables the
next day, the ponies were grazing in the
sunshine, their tails lazily swishing at the
flies. There was not even a breath of
wind to move the leaves on the trees
and the skies were cloudless. The air
seemed so still it was almost creepy.
Erin felt a prickle of unease. She was
glad it was clear, but why was it like
this? Surely Marianne had started using
Mistral to control the skies by now. In

which case, shouldn't the weather be stormy? And, even if Marianne wasn't using Mistral, why were the horses in the skies not more agitated now that Tor and Mistral were on Earth?

In one way, she felt very glad the weather was so calm. It would be awful for there to be a big storm and for her not to have learnt enough about weather weaving to be able to sort things out. But it did seem strange.

She wished Chloe was there to talk to about it, but she had already gone to Devon. It was weird being at the stables without her that day. Fran and Katie kept whispering together and glancing at her all morning. She was sure they were talking about Kestrel running off with her the day before.

Erin managed to stay out of their way until lunchtime, when she walked past the two girls filling up the water buckets. She saw Fran move the hosepipe out the corner of her eye, but wasn't quick enough to miss being sprayed all over her jodhpurs and trainers.

As Erin exclaimed in shock, Jackie came out of a stable. She hadn't noticed what had just happened. 'Ah, Erin. I thought all the helpers could go out for a ride in the fields this afternoon. Would you like to ride Kestrel?'

Erin felt her stomach fill with ice. 'Um . . .' She could feel Fran and Katie watching her curiously.

'I'll lunge him first so he'll be quite quiet,' Jackie said reassuringly. 'I do think it would be good for you to ride him again.'

Pictures flashed through Erin's mind: Kestrel veering round the corner, the looks on everyone's faces, the feeling of being unable to stop. She couldn't do it! 'I . . . I don't want to!' she burst out.

Jackie looked at her in surprise. 'I know you had a bad experience yesterday, but I really think you should get on him again.'

'No,' Erin insisted, wanting to sink into the ground.

Jackie frowned. 'Well, all right. I won't force you. You can ride one of the others today, but I'd like you to ride him again soon.'

She walked off.

Fran and Katie giggled, and Erin hurried away, her feet wet in her trainers, her face burning. *Oh, Chloe,* she thought miserably, *I wish you were here.*

That night when Erin arrived in the woods, she found Tor pacing uneasily around. 'The skies are very clear,' he said, looking upwards.

'I know,' said Erin. 'I thought you said that now Marianne had Mistral there would be really bad weather.'

'I thought there would be.' Tor pawed the ground anxiously. 'Something isn't right. Have you brought the stones with you?'

Erin nodded. After her experience the day before, she wasn't looking forward to using a seeing stone again. She took two grey stones out of the pocket of her dress and held them out. The stallion investigated them. 'A warding stone to protect with,' he said, touching the stone with two holes with his muzzle. 'And a seeing stone to see with,' he said, touching the stone with the single hole. 'We will start with the warding stone,' he said, to Erin's relief. 'Was this one of your mother's stones?'

Erin nodded.

'Good. In weather weaving, family links are extremely important,' Tor said. 'If your mother has worked spells of protection with this stone, then it will have absorbed some of her magic and if you add your own magic on top by working with it too, it will become more powerful than it would otherwise have been.'

Erin stared at the stone, thinking of what her mother might have done with it before her. 'So how does the magic work?' she asked.

'Each type of hagstone has a different kind of magic inside it and you, being a weather weaver, have the ability to free that power and use it,' Tor explained. 'The way in which you free a stone's power is the same regardless of the type of hagstone. Try now. Hold the warding stone with both hands. Imagine sinking into it and you will feel magic flowing through your fingers. As you feel the magic, you must focus on what you want the stone to do.' He pushed her with his muzzle. 'A warding stone can give protection so imagine that nothing and no one is able to touch or hurt you.'

Erin held the stone in her hands and looked down at it. It was a pale grey with shards chipped off it, showing a darker grey underneath the surface layers.

The two holes in the centre were full of dark shadows. She stared into the two holes and felt a strange dissolving sensation, almost as if she was sinking into the stone. Her fingers started to buzz. The buzzing spread throughout her whole body.

'Focus on what you want,' Tor's voice said softly in the background.

Erin imagined an invisible shield all around her. She imagined rocks being thrown at her, but bouncing away, not being able to hurt her. She imagined Marianne casting spells at her, but the spells glancing off like the rocks. Suddenly the stone turned icy in her hands.

'The stone!' she said. 'It's gone cold!'

'That means the magic is working,'

Tor told her. He reared up and struck at an overhanging branch with his front hooves. It cracked and fell away from the tree, cannoning through the air, straight towards Erin. She cried out in alarm and ducked, but just as the branch was about to hit her it seemed to bounce away, leaving her unharmed.

'Good,' Tor whinnied approvingly. 'You have made the stone work very well.'

Erin felt relieved and amazed at what she had just done. 'Does that mean so long as I carry this stone I'll be OK?' she asked.

'The protection will wear off,' Tor said. 'You must keep renewing it. How long it lasts depends upon the strength of your magic. And you must still be

careful,' he added, as if reading the
thoughts that were running through
her mind about how brilliant it would
be to feel that no one and nothing
could hurt her. 'You will have a certain
level of protection, but it will not be
enough to protect you if Marianne
turns the full force of her magic
against you. One day, after a lot of
practice, you will be able to protect
yourself against a dark spirit like her,
but at the moment, although a warding
stone will help you, it will not protect
you completely.'

Erin's excitement faded slightly.

'Now, let's use a seeing stone. Work
with it in the same way. Let your magic
sink into it and try seeing something or
someone – although not Marianne, of

course,' Tor said, nudging the seeing stone with his nose.

Erin picked the seeing stone up slowly. Tendrils of fear curled at the edges of her mind. What if she saw Marianne by mistake?

Maybe she would try to see Chloe. Yes. She focused her thoughts on her friend. *Think Chloe*, she thought. But as she felt the buzzing in her fingers a persistent picture of Marianne filled her mind. Panic rose inside her and she lowered the stone.

'What's the matter?' Tor asked.

'N-nothing,' Erin said. 'I'll try again.'

Come on, she told herself. *You can do this.*

'Just let your magic flow,' Tor said softly.

But every time the magic started to tingle through her she thought of Marianne and pulled away from the stone.

'I can't do it!' she exclaimed after half an hour. 'I just can't do it any more!'

Tor looked troubled. 'I know it is frightening, but you must overcome your fears, Erin. In order to break the trapping stone you will have to cast a vision using a seeing stone as well. It is vitally important you can do it, Erin.'

'I will be able to,' Erin promised. 'I'm sure I will. Just not now. Can I try again tomorrow?'

Tor nodded. 'I will see you tomorrow evening then.'

As Erin flew out of the woods, a mixture of feelings flowed through her – frustration, worry, an underlying relief that she hadn't had to deal with looking into a vision.

But you have to if you want to break the trapping stone and free Mistral, she told herself, remembering what Tor had just said.

She swallowed. If she couldn't do it, the foal would never be free.

You have to do it, she thought. *You just have to!*

Seven

Chloe got back from Devon the next day and came to the stables at lunchtime. 'I had a brilliant time last night,' she whispered to Erin. 'How about you?'

'It wasn't great,' Erin admitted. 'I made the warding stone work, but I couldn't do anything with the seeing stone. What did you get up to?'

'I can't wait to tell you all about it. I learnt how to –' Chloe broke off as

Jackie came over. 'I'll show you tonight,' she said quickly. 'Meet me at the beach.'

They didn't get a chance to talk stardust stuff at all for the rest of the day. There were always too many people around and Jackie kept them busy cleaning tack and mucking out stables. There wasn't even time to do any riding, but for once Erin didn't mind because it meant that she didn't have to think of an excuse for not riding Kestrel.

Although she wasn't looking forward to having another try at working with a seeing stone that night, she flew towards the beach feeling excited. What was Chloe going to show her?

The beach where they usually met was near the spit of land where the three rocks of World's End stood. As Erin flew over the cliff top towards it, she saw Chloe sitting on a rock below her. Chloe's eyes were fixed on the shingle in front of her where there was a small fire burning brightly. Erin watched as Chloe lifted her right hand and moved it in a circle in the air. The flames from the fire also began to curl into a circle.

'Oh wow!' Erin gasped as the flames formed a ball.

Chloe jumped. The flames immediately sank back down again.

'That was brilliant!' said Erin. 'How did you do it?'

Chloe looked pleased. 'Just with my magic. I'm not very good at it yet. Allegra and her friends can make loads of different shapes. They showed me yesterday. Allegra made the wind make a tornado shape, and Lucy and Robyn, Allegra's friends, made balls of fire turn into columns and pyramids. I can only make a ball shape at the moment, but I'm going to practise and practise until I can make all sorts of different shapes too.'

'What do you have to do?' Erin said.

'You just imagine the fire or whatever becoming a different shape and move your hand in that shape. Any stardust spirit can do it.'

Erin was keen to try. She pointed at the sky. 'Rain be with me!' Almost immediately a small raincloud formed and raindrops started falling. Chloe squealed as some landed on her bare skin. Erin hastily steered the cloud away from them. She tried to imagine the water flowing in a circle instead of falling down and she moved her hand as she had seen Chloe doing.

It worked! The rain twisted up before it reached the ground, and swirled in a circle, making a ball of water in the sky.

'Cool!' Chloe exclaimed.

Magic seemed to glance off the water, sending glowing multicoloured drops sparkling through the air. Erin grinned in delight. 'This is fun!'

She made the ball bigger. As it grew, it got thinner and more see-through in the centre. *It could almost be a hagstone*, she thought. *Maybe I could make it into a hagstone shape . . .* Concentrating hard, she imagined the ball of water in the

air having a hole through its centre.
Gradually the water moved and shifted
until it was forming the shape of a
hagstone.

'Hey, that looks good!' Chloe said.

Erin felt her fingertips start to buzz
just as they did if she was holding a real
hagstone. She could feel the hole
starting to draw her towards it.

'It feels like it's magic,' she said.

'Of course it's magic!' Chloe grinned.

'No, not normal magic,' Erin said, trying to explain. 'Weather-weaving magic.'

As she stopped concentrating, the water hagstone dissolved and started to fall as rain again.

'Rain be gone!' said Erin, and the rain stopped.

'I'm going to try again,' said Chloe.

They practised for half an hour until they were both quicker at forming shapes and then they set off to see Tor. On the way Chloe told Erin about the other things she had done the night before. 'There are loads of stardust spirits who meet in the woods there,' she said. 'It's brilliant. The best bit was meeting all

Allegra's friends who are stardust spirits too. They're great. You'll have to come with me one day!'

'I'd love to!' said Erin. She thought it sounded amazing. She sighed. 'You had much more fun than me.' She shook her head. 'Whenever I try to use a seeing stone to cast a vision, I just see Marianne in my mind and have to stop, but Tor said that if I'm going to break the trapping stone I'm going to have to cast a vision.' She sighed. 'But we've also got to find the trapping stone. We're no closer to working out where Marianne is keeping it.'

Chloe gave her a sympathetic look. 'We'll find it. I know we will. And don't worry about the visions. I'm sure you'll be able to cast one soon – you've done it before.'

But that was different. Now it feels like Marianne is waiting for me, Erin thought. She sighed and together they headed to the woods.

Tor was waiting for them. He listened carefully as they told him what they had been doing with their stardust magic on the beach.

'Let me see,' he said.

Erin didn't need any encouraging. It might not help them find Mistral, but it felt good – easy – doing this type of magic. Not scary at all. She conjured up a raincloud and as the rain started to fall she did what she had done on the beach and imagined the rain forming a hagstone shape in the sky.

The water swirled round; it seemed to flash with colour, blue then green then purple. Erin felt her hands start to tingle; the darkness in the hole grew. She heard Tor whinny behind her.

'A seeing stone made of water! Oh, Erin, this is just what we need!'

'What do you mean?' Erin heard Chloe say.

Tor stamped a front hoof. 'This is how we can watch Marianne without danger!'

Erin was so surprised that she swung round. The water hagstone dissolved instantly. 'What?' she asked, moving back as raindrops splashed from the ground over her legs.

'You've done it! You have discovered

a way to find Mistral!' exclaimed the stallion.

Erin looked at him in astonishment. 'But how?'

Tor nuzzled her hair. 'You can use your weather-weaving powers to watch safely through a seeing stone made of water. The dark spirit will not be able to sense you or harm you because you will be watching her using water, not stone. And, because you are using a different element, her warding hagstone will not warn her. Oh, cleverest weather weaver! I should have thought of this.'

Chloe frowned. 'But I don't get it. Don't weather weavers use the magic that's in the hagstones themselves? This isn't a stone; it's just water.'

'And so it is the purest, most

powerful magic. Water is the most magical element of all,' said Tor. 'It creates hagstones. All hagstones start as normal stones, but as water flows around them the holes in them are formed. It is the water that gives them their magic in the first place.'

'So all I need to do is make a water hagstone and use it like a seeing stone,' Erin said. 'And then I might be able to see Marianne without her seeing me.'

Tor nodded. 'You will be safe.'

'Then I'll do it now.' Erin's heart leapt. She looked at the raincloud and imagined the rain turning into a hagstone again.

'Focus your magic,' Tor reminded her quickly. 'Think very carefully about what you want to see.'

Erin stared at the hole in the water hagstone.

The trapping stone with Mistral . . .

The world seemed to swim slightly in front of her. Magic sparkled through her whole body as the dark hole at the centre of the water hagstone seemed to grow. For a moment she remembered Marianne trapping her before, but Tor had said that wouldn't happen this time. *I believe him*, she thought. *I want to do this.* And she let the darkness swell out and claim her.

The trapping stone, the trapping stone, she thought over and over again.

All she could see was the inky blackness, but gradually it began to move apart like dark curtains and she could see a picture behind it. It was a

cave like she'd seen before. She let
herself move towards it and suddenly
she was there. Inside the cave. But it
wasn't like before when she had felt as
if she really was there. This time it felt
as if she was just floating without a
body. Her bones felt cold, as though she
was soaking in freezing water. She
could see the damp on the walls. On
the floor there was a circle made out of

stones and chalk. There were rocky ledges around the cave and on them there were white candles, but all of them were unlit. She could hear the waves below the cave dragging on shingle.

It must be a cave by the beach, she realized.

She floated towards the entrance. It wasn't a cave at ground level. She was high up a cliff. But from here she could see the top of three shadowy rocks on a spit of land – two tall, one round with a hole in its centre. Waves were breaking around them, spray flying up into the air and glittering in the starlight.

World's End! The thought came to Erin. *It's a cave near World's End!*

She looked around the cave again. It was cold and silent inside. She shivered, the hair prickling at the back of her neck. Where was the trapping stone? It must be here if the vision had showed her this place. Her eyes caught sight of a natural rocky alcove at the very back of the cave. It was like an open-fronted cupboard. There were some objects in it. She went over.

A bowl of water, a candle, a jar of earth and a bottle with nothing in it.

And something else. A piece of paper with writing on. Erin tried to pick it up, but her fingers passed straight through it. She couldn't touch or move anything. All she could do was look. She read the first line on the paper:

When the dark one returns, the door shall be reopened . . .

It was the prophecy again! The same one that was in her mum's box and the same one that Marianne had spoken when she had trapped Mistral. But there seemed to be more of it on this piece of paper. Another two verses! Erin was about to read on when a noise behind her suddenly made her swing round. She caught her breath in horror – Marianne was standing in the cave entrance!

Eight

For a moment, Erin felt herself freeze, but then she realized that Marianne was looking around the cave *and couldn't see her*!

Marianne pulled a shining ball from the pocket of her black cloak and held it out in front of her. The candles immediately lit up. Shadows flickered over the cave walls.

With a swish of her silvery-blue dress, Marianne strode towards the back of the cave. Erin quickly slipped round to the right. 'Three days out of six,' the dark spirit muttered. 'Just three more and then the fourth stone will appear!' She reached into the alcove and from the very back drew out a hagstone.

Erin stared at it. It was the trapping stone! It was light brown and had a chip of rock in the middle of it. She watched as Marianne placed it in the centre of the circle and then put the other four objects that had been in the alcove around it. She lit the candle and then took two stones out of her pocket and placed one on either side of her. A warding stone and a seeing stone, Erin noticed. Marianne knelt down and clapped her hands. 'Appear!'

Cloud flowed out of the stone and

formed into the shape of a miniature
grey foal, no bigger than one of the toy
plastic horses Erin had at home. His
legs were streaked with dried blood, his
mane and tail were tangled, his head
hung low.

Mistral! Erin desperately wanted to
scoop him up. He looked utterly
bewildered and frightened.

'It is time to begin again, Prince,'
Marianne hissed. 'Another day of clear
skies.'

She clapped her hands again and the
horse moved to the edge of the circle.
He walked around it almost as if
guarding a boundary. For one moment,
Erin thought she saw the misty shape
of another horse begin to appear at the
edge of the circle. The colt rushed at it,

ears pinned back and the shape melted away. Erin was utterly mystified. What was going on?

When every horse who appeared at the edge of the circle had been sent away, Marianne clapped her hands. The colt turned back to mist and was sucked back into the stone.

'Day four begins . . .' the dark weather weaver whispered to herself.

Erin decided it was time to go. Her head was spinning with everything she had seen. None of it seemed to make any sense. She shut her eyes and imagined herself back in the woods with Chloe and Tor. She felt herself falling and then suddenly felt ground beneath her. Her fingers clutched at it. Feeling grass and twigs, she blinked her eyes open. She was back in the woods! Chloe was crouching anxiously beside her. Tor was watching intently.

'Erin!' Chloe said as Erin opened her eyes. 'Are you OK?'

Erin nodded. For a moment she couldn't speak. It was too weird to have been in one place, to see it so clearly, and then to wake up and find herself somewhere else. 'I'm all right,' she said slowly. She realized she was lying on the ground and she sat up. The water hagstone had turned to rain. 'Rain be gone!' she whispered. The cloud disappeared instantly.

'That was horrible. One minute you were standing up looking at the water hagstone and the next you just collapsed on the ground,' Chloe said.

'Tor said you were OK, that you were in a vision, but you were just lying there. The water hagstone stayed until you opened your eyes and then it just turned to rain again before you got rid of the cloud. Are you really all right?'

Erin nodded.

'The trapping stone,' Tor said, stepping forward, his voice urgent. 'Did you see where it was hidden, Erin?'

'Yes.' Erin took a deep breath. 'It's in

a cave near World's End. I saw it and I saw Marianne using it.'

'You saw the dark one?' Tor breathed. 'And Mistral?'

'Yes, I saw him. I watched Marianne summon him.' Erin shook her head, trying to push away the horrible vision of the exhausted, confused colt in the chalk circle. 'We have to rescue him, Tor!'

'Now we know where the cave is, we can go there,' Chloe said. 'Then you can use your magic to break the trapping stone and free Mistral.'

Erin swallowed. She knew that was what she had to do, but she felt so exhausted just by what she had done that night. She remembered the eerie feeling in the cave and the power that seemed to spark off Marianne.

Tor breathed gently on her face and neck. As his warm breath brushed over her skin, she felt better. She touched his solid neck, her fingers curling in his soft mane.

'You did well,' he told her softly. 'Did the dark one say anything? Did you see what she was trying to do?'

'Yes, but I just don't get it. She said, "Clear the skies."' Erin described what had happened, trying not to miss anything out. 'Mistral just walked round and round as if guarding the circle,' she said. 'And then Marianne put him back in the stone and said something about it being day four.'

'Day four!' Tor stamped a front hoof on the ground. 'So *that* is what she is trying to do! I should have realized sooner,' he said. 'The cloudless skies, the fact that Mistral couldn't possibly be resisting a spirit with her powers. I should have understood that Marianne was trying to reveal the fourth stone.'

Erin eyes widened. 'But what is the fourth stone?'

'There is a fourth rock at World's End,' Tor explained. 'It is not a real rock any more than a water hagstone is a real stone. It looks like a giant hagstone, but is made out of water. It is hidden below the waves and appears after six days of complete calm and cloudless skies.'

Erin suddenly remembered where else she had heard the words *fourth stone*. 'Aunt Alice told me that World's End used to be called Four Rocks. Is that why?'

Tor nodded. 'It is written in the stars that if a weather weaver passes a hagstone tied with their hair through the hole in the fourth rock they will then have all the power they need to control the weather without keeping a sky horse captive. That is what Marianne must be trying to do. For now, she is succeeding in using Mistral to control the weather, but she must know that as he gets older he will fight her more and more. This way would allow her to have complete power without him.'

'If day four has just started, then we've only got two more days to stop her!' said Erin in alarm.

'But we could ruin her plans easily!'

said Chloe. 'You could use the seeing stone to cast a vision of Tor into the skies and he could make the weather stormy!'

'But I can't do visions like that at the moment,' Erin protested.

'And anyway it would be very dangerous for Mistral if we did that while he is in the dark one's power,' Tor put in. 'I do not like to think what she might do to him in revenge against us for stopping her plans.'

'I hadn't thought of that,' Chloe admitted. 'But at least we know where Marianne is keeping the trapping stone now. We can get it, then you can work the magic that will break it, Erin.'

'But what if I can't do it?' said Erin anxiously. 'I have to be able to cast visions to do that.' She had an idea and turned to Tor, hope flaring through her suddenly as she had an idea. 'Could I use a water hagstone to cast the vision that is needed to break the trapping stone?'

'No,' he answered heavily. 'The vision you will need to cast has to be made using a real stone. If you were an older or more experienced weather weaver, you could do it without going into a vision, but you are still too new at this. When you

are in a vision, your magic is in its
strongest, most concentrated form. If
you cannot do it, then the stone will
not break and Mistral will stay trapped
forever.'

Erin felt a wave of cold. So she had to
cast a vision using a real hagstone. 'Oh.'

'You will be able to do it,' Chloe told
her quickly. 'Why don't you have
another try now?'

Erin reluctantly took a seeing stone
out of her pocket. She held it in her
hands.

'Just remember not to think of
Marianne,' said Tor.

But as Erin stared at the dark centre,
she found she couldn't think of
anything else. What if Marianne was
waiting for her and used a seeing stone

of her own to pull her into a vision? What if this time she didn't escape?

Her fingers started to tingle, darkness clouded the edges of her sight and the hole seemed to grow.

No!

Erin recoiled.

'What's the matter?' Chloe demanded.

'I can't do it,' Erin stammered. 'I don't want to!'

Tor breathed on her hair. 'You can. Please, Erin. Try again.'

Erin felt awful. 'OK.' But although she tried and tried, she just couldn't do it. It was like there was a barrier there. As if something was stopping her. Every time she felt herself falling, her mind seemed to pull her back.

'I can't do it,' she said again.

Tor sighed. 'We must leave it for now.' He glanced at the sky, which was starting to look a paler grey. 'Dawn is coming. Tomorrow we will go to the cave and get the trapping stone. Hopefully the dark one will not be there, but even if she is we have no time to lose. I will provide a distraction, giving you the chance to get into the cave and take it. When we have the stone you must try to cast a vision.'

'We'll see you tomorrow night, Tor,' said Chloe, rising into the air.

'Bye, Tor,' said Erin, forcing a smile.

But as she flew with Chloe the smile quickly faded from her face.

Chloe glanced at her. 'It'll be OK.'

Erin swallowed. She really hoped Chloe was right.

CHAPTER

Nine

'So what have you got planned for today?' asked Jo brightly as Erin got into the passenger seat of the car the next morning.

'Nothing much,' sighed Erin. She thought about the day ahead. No doubt Fran and Katie would be laughing at her as usual, and then in the evening . . . well, she didn't want to think about that.

They drove towards the stables. 'Have

you ridden that new pony yet?' Jo
asked. 'The one you were talking about
the other day.'

Erin hesitated. 'Kestrel? Kind of.'

Jo raised her eyebrows. 'Kind of?'

'I rode him the other day.' Erin
looked at her stepmother's kind face
and sighed as she admitted the truth. 'It
was awful, Jo. He cantered off with me.
Jackie says I should ride him again, but
I don't want to.' She glanced at Jo,
wondering how she would react.

To her relief, her stepmum gave her a
sympathetic look. 'That must be tough.
Are you getting teased about it?'

Erin nodded. 'Yeah. A bit.' Her voice
dropped miserably. 'I . . . I wish I was
braver. More like Chloe. She's not
scared of anything.'

Jo glanced at her. 'Being brave isn't about not feeling scared; it's about doing something even though it scares you.'

Erin frowned. She hadn't thought about it like that. But even if it was true it still didn't really help her. She was too afraid to ride Kestrel again.

'You know there are times when I'm windsurfing with your dad and the boys and I want to try something, but I feel scared because it's new and difficult,' Jo went on. 'However, if I do try, I always feel good about myself. Even if I make a complete mess, even if I fall off and look really stupid and your dad and the boys laugh, I still feel better because I know I tried. I always feel dreadful if I don't. Maybe you should try riding

Kestrel again. Even if he runs off with
you, at least you'll feel better knowing
you were brave enough to have a
go.'

'Maybe,' Erin muttered.

Jo reached across and squeezed her
arm. 'I promise it's always better to face
your fears and not let them control
you.'

Erin didn't say anything and they
drove the rest of the way in silence.

'I hope today's OK,' said Jo as she
stopped the car at the stables.

'Thanks,' sighed Erin, and got out of the car.

'So, Erin, are you going to ride Kestrel today?' asked Fran with a smirk as Erin fetched a grooming kit from the tack room that morning.

Katie giggled. 'Or are you going to be too scared?'

Fran pretended to imitate Erin. 'Oh, please, Jackie, don't make me ride that horrible, nasty pony. I'm such a little baby.'

Erin's cheeks burnt as she walked out of the tack room.

Chloe was waiting beside the water trough. 'Jackie says can we get Kestrel and Tango in from the lower field before we start grooming. She said we can ride them back.' She saw Erin's face. 'It's OK. I'll ride Kestrel. You can ride Tango. But I don't know why you're still being so funny about Kestrel. He's been really quiet ever since that day you rode him.'

Erin felt a wave of misery. Now even Chloe thought she was being silly. *Great*, she thought unhappily.

They got their hard hats and the ponies' bridles and walked down to the lower field. It was the furthest field from the stables. They had to walk up the gravel drive that led to the stables and turn off down a path. 'Look, at least catch Kestrel,' said Chloe when they reached the field gate. 'I'll ride him back, but just lead him in from the field.'

'OK,' agreed Erin, not wanting Chloe

to change her mind about letting her ride Tango. Anyway, she didn't mind leading Kestrel at all; it was just the thought of riding him that made her feel sick. She found some Polos in her pocket and caught him easily. Putting his bridle on, she led him up the field and took him through the gate.

Tango was right at the bottom of the field. Chloe vaulted on and trotted the round chestnut pony up to the gate. 'This is cool!' she called. 'This way I get to ride both of them!'

Erin had left the gate unbolted. Chloe leant over and pulled it open. Seeing Kestrel on the other side, Tango walked eagerly through, but as he did so the gate started to swing shut.

'Watch out, Chloe!' cried Erin.

Chloe saw that they were about to get trapped, and kicked Tango on. But it was too late. The edge of the gate banged into Tango's body. The chestnut pony plunged forward in alarm and as he did so the gate caught on Chloe's leg. She lost her balance and fell off with a cry. Erin gasped as Tango headed towards her.

'Stop him, Erin!' Chloe yelled from the ground.

Erin made a wild grab for the reins, but Tango swerved past her and cantered on down the path.

'He'll get on to the drive!' Chloe shrieked. 'What if there's a car? He'll be run over!'

Erin hesitated for a split second. Tango had slowed to a trot, but was still heading for the drive, the reins flapping dangerously around his legs. She had to stop him. There was only one way.

She looked desperately at Kestrel. *I can't do it*, she thought, feeling sick. *I have to*, she realized.

Heart hammering and hands sweating, she got on to the fence and jumped on to Kestrel's back.

Her legs had barely touched his sides when the grey pony leapt forward, but Erin was so focused on catching Tango that she hardly had time to be scared. 'Come on, boy!' she urged, leaning forward.

Kestrel flew along the grassy path after Tango. The chestnut pony heard his hooves and broke into a canter again, but Kestrel was already drawing alongside him. Gripping hard with her knees, Erin leant over and grabbed at Tango's reins. Her hands closed on the leather.

'Whoa!' she gasped, sitting back and pulling both ponies' reins as hard as she could. Kestrel bounced to a stop and so did Tango.

'Erin! You did it! You stopped him!'

Erin looked round. Chloe was racing down the path towards her.

A grin of pure relief spread across Erin's face.

Reaching her, Chloe threw her arms round Tango's neck. 'Oh, Tango! I thought you were going to be hurt!' She swung round. 'Erin! You rode Kestrel!'

Erin felt as if every bit of her body was humming; it was like doing the best type of magic. 'He was brilliant, weren't you, boy?' she said, hugging Kestrel.

'You were *both* brilliant!' Chloe exclaimed. 'Guess you're not going to be scared of riding him again now.'

Erin shook her head. She didn't think she'd ever felt happier.

Chloe mounted and the two of them rode back to the stables.

When they got to the yard, Jackie saw them. 'Erin! You're riding Kestrel!'

'Yep,' said Erin, still grinning.

'That's great.' Jackie looked very pleased. 'I was starting to get worried about you not riding him. Would you like to ride him in the jumping lesson this afternoon?'

For a moment Erin felt a flicker of her old fear, but she remembered what

Jo had said in the car about having a go and she forced the fear down. 'Yes, please,' she said, patting Kestrel's neck.

Erin was a bit nervous, but the afternoon jumping lesson was great. Kestrel did everything she asked and when they had a timed mini-jumping competition at the end he won.

'Well done!' Chloe told her, as they rode the ponies out of the ring at the end. 'You were great, Erin!'

Fran and Katie rode past them.

'Didn't Erin ride Kestrel well?' Chloe called out with a grin.

They both scowled and ignored her.

Erin and Chloe burst into giggles. Erin stopped Kestrel and dismounted with a happy sigh. She felt as if a huge

weight had lifted from her shoulders.
She hugged Kestrel. 'You're the best
pony in the world,' she told him. 'The
very best.' She thought of Tor. She loved
him so much too, but he was a majestic
stallion from another world and
sometimes it was
just lovely to be
with a pony you
could hug and
cuddle.

Kestrel
rubbed his
head against
her, leaving
a trail of
green foam
from his
mouth on

her T-shirt and then snorted all over her too for good measure.

'Thanks, Kestrel!' Erin said, grinning. She couldn't imagine Tor doing that!

Erin and Chloe had arranged to meet in the woods that night. Erin was the first to get there. Tor was waiting for her. As she landed, he stepped forward with a low whicker.

'Hi.' Erin cautiously patted his neck. As she stroked him, he lifted his muzzle to her face. His eyes looked worried. Erin wondered if he was anxious about the night ahead of them.

Of course he is, she realized. Tor, like her, knew just how powerful a dark spirit such as Marianne was. He still had the mark on his neck where

Marianne's binding rope had cut into him, leaving raw wounds, and he was desperately worried about his son.

But, strangely, the thought that he was worried didn't actually make Erin feel worse. She looked into Tor's troubled eyes and felt suddenly brave. 'It'll be OK, Tor,' she said softly. 'We'll get the trapping stone and I'll cast the vision and set Mistral free and then you'll both go through the gateway back to the clouds.'

'I hope so.' The stallion rested his muzzle on her shoulder.

'What will I have to do when I'm in the vision?' Erin asked.

'Water made the trapping stone what it is and water can also destroy it. You must use your stardust magic to call up

rain,' Tor told her. 'You must make the
rain flow through the hole in the centre
of the trapping stone. If you succeed, the
stone will break. When the stone splits, I
will do the rest.'

Erin tried to stop the shiver that ran
through her at the idea of casting a
vision.

For a moment they stood in silence,
both lost in thought.

'Hi!' called Chloe, flying down
through the trees, breaking the quiet.

Tor stepped back.

'Sorry I'm late. Mum and Dad took
ages to go to bed.' Chloe landed, her
eyes alight and excited. 'I've mailed
Xanthe and told her we might be about
to get the trapping stone. So what's the
plan for tonight?'

Tor snorted. 'First Erin should check to see if Marianne is in the cave. We have to get the trapping stone tonight so, even if she is, we must go there and I will try to distract her while you two slip into the cave and take it.'

'And then Erin does her magic and breaks it,' said Chloe, glancing at Erin. 'After that, will Mistral be free to go back to the sky with you?'

'Not quite. But I will do the rest,' Tor answered.

Erin wondered what he meant. When Mistral had first been trapped, Tor had refused to go back to the sky without him because he said only he could speak the colt's cloud name to finally free him from Marianne's control. Was that what he meant?

Before she could ask, Tor carried on
speaking. 'We have no time to waste.
We must get the trapping stone. Erin,
can you use a water hagstone now to
see if Marianne is at the cave.'

Erin quickly conjured up a raincloud
and turned it into a water hagstone. She
used it to cast a vision of the cave. It was
dark and empty. 'She's not there yet!' Erin
said, coming out of her vision.

'Then let's go – and quickly!' Tor
reared up. Erin caught her breath as he

changed into his cloud form. His white coat sparkled like early morning mist, his body becoming slightly cloudy and ghost-like. He plunged forward and set off through the trees.

Erin and Chloe raced after him. As they all burst out of the woods, Tor cantered into the sky, his mane and tail swirling around him as he joined the girls. They swooped over the headland until they saw the three rocks at World's End silhouetted against the sky. The hagstone and the two tall stones. *Almost like fingers pointing up at the cloud world,* Erin thought.

'Camouflage yourselves,' warned Tor. 'I will wait in case Marianne comes. If she does, I will distract her so that you can escape. Be as quick as you can.'

'We will,' promised Erin. She had no intention of hanging around.

She and Chloe whispered the word '*camouflagus*' and their bodies faded into the background. They flew over the edge of the cliff. Erin could feel Chloe beside her even though she couldn't see her any more.

'Where do you think the cave might be?' whispered Chloe as they flew parallel with the cliff. Below them the waves were breaking on the rocks. Sea spray flew into the air, falling on their skin. Behind stood the rocks of World's End like enormous stone guards.

Erin scanned the shadowy cliff face. When she'd been in the cave in her vision, she'd just been able to see the top of the stones at World's End. She flew a bit lower. Where was the cave? Suddenly she saw a large dark hole, half hidden behind a jutting rock. 'It's here!' she hissed.

'Let's go in,' said Chloe.

A thought struck Erin. 'But what if Marianne has got here since I looked in the water hagstone? What if she's inside it right now?'

'There's only one way to find out!' Chloe flew towards the cave.

'Wait!' gasped Erin, but Chloe had disappeared through the entrance.

CHAPTER

Ten

Erin dashed after Chloe. The entrance
was narrow and she had to turn
sideways to slip round the rock. As she
flew into the cave, she tensed, but then
immediately felt a rush of relief. There
was no sign of Marianne.

'Chloe?' she whispered, peering
through the cold, inky blackness.

'I'm here,' replied Chloe, just to her
left. 'It's really dark and creepy.'

'There are some candles around the

walls,' said Erin, remembering her vision. 'If we had some matches, we could light one.'

'Who needs matches?' There was the sound of Chloe fumbling around the walls. 'Got one!' she said. 'Fire be with me!'

The wick of the candle she had picked up burst into flame. Its flame

was small, but it cast just enough light
to let Erin see through the gloom. She
saw the circle on the floor and her skin
prickled as she remembered watching
Marianne commanding the foal when
he had been inside it.

She glanced at Chloe, who had
dropped her camouflage and was
putting the candle back on the ledge.
'Let's get the trapping stone as quickly
as we can.'

'It's over here, I think,' said Erin,
flying to the back of the cave. She
found the alcove and reached inside.
Her fingers felt a bottle, a bowl, a piece
of paper . . .

She pulled the paper out. It was the
piece of paper she had seen in her
vision. With everything else that had

been happening, she had forgotten
about it, but as she read the first line –
*When the dark one returns, the door shall
be reopened* – she felt a shiver run down
her spine. Her eyes swept quickly down
the page:

*When the dark one returns, the door shall
   be reopened
And danger will threaten all living below.
If the binding is broken, they can be
   protected,
But one coming willingly lets the dark's
   power grow
Until the first gateway is split by magic
And he who is trapped is free to go.*

*Two gateways now balance the light and
   the darkness,*

One lost in memory, hidden by the sea.
The dark door is reserved for the hand
  that creates it.
The other lies close to a whispering tree,
Deep underground and made from
  moonlight.
When it is found, then two can be free.

Yet danger is found with the new
  gateway –
Beware the dark horse who leaps for the
  sky.
With arrow of fire and grey feather's
  direction,
Two must help here or all hopes will die.
If the darkest impostor is not defeated,
Then never again will the cloud stallion
  fly.

Erin stared at it. What did it all mean? What were the gateways it was going on about?

'Erin! What are you doing?' hissed Chloe urgently.

Erin shoved the paper into her pocket. There was no time to think about it now. She reached further into the hole. She felt a glass jar and then . . . yes, there it was! Her hand closed round a stone. She pulled it out and saw in the dim light that it was the brown trapping stone with the chip of rock through the centre. Her heart lifted. 'I've got it!' She swung round to Chloe. Maybe things were going to be OK. Maybe they were going to take the stone without Marianne seeing them . . .

'Let's get out of here!' Chloe said.

'We'd better camouflage ourselves again just in case Marianne is heading this way,' called Erin.

They both muttered, '*Camouflagus*,' and disappeared.

But just as they reached the cave entrance they heard a voice outside. 'Sky stallion! What are you doing here?'

Erin froze. It was Marianne.

There was a wild whinny. 'I have come to rescue my son!'

'Marianne's outside!' hissed Erin in alarm. 'What are we going to do?'

There was a moment's silence. 'Keep camouflaged,' said Chloe, thinking fast. 'And try to sneak out while Marianne's talking to Tor. As soon as we're out, we have to get away with the trapping stone. We'll hide between the rocks down there and you can try and cast the vision to free Mistral.'

'But what about Tor?' asked Erin.

'We'll have to start without him,' said Chloe as they heard another whinny from outside. 'Come on!'

The two girls edged round the rock, holding hands. *Keep camouflaged, keep camouflaged*, Erin told herself frantically.

She stifled a gasp as they emerged. Marianne was in the sky, hovering only a few metres away from them, and she was facing Tor. 'You cannot stop me, sky stallion!' She raised her hands. 'I am going to get to the fourth stone and I will use your son to do it.'

Tor plunged forward with a furious squeal. He grew as he leapt, his cloud shape getting bigger, seeming to fill the sky. He struck out with his front hooves.

Marianne recoiled. 'Bind him!' she snapped out, pointing her hands at him as he landed in the space where she had been flying.

White cobwebby ropes of mist appeared out of nowhere and wound around the stallion. Tor struggled, lashing out with his forelegs, but the ropes coiled like cruel snakes, holding him fast.

Marianne twisted one hand in the air and the ropes got tighter and tighter. Tor struggled, but one of the ropes slithered around his neck, behind his ears, and then down between his legs, pulling his head low.

Erin couldn't bear it. She flew forward.

'NO!' hissed Chloe in her ear, pulling her back hard. 'We can't help him, Erin! Marianne is too strong for us to fight.'

'We can't just leave him!' cried Erin, watching in despair as the ropes pulled Tor down to his knees in the sky, and Marianne laughed harshly.

'We have to!' Chloe squeezed her hand hard. 'It's what he would tell us to do! We have to free Mistral!'

The next thing Erin knew, Chloe had grabbed the stone from her and set off!

Erin hesitated. Tor's ears were flattened against his head, his eyes furious. She hated leaving him, but Chloe was right. She had to try to break the trapping stone! It was the only way to end this.

Erin raced after Chloe, down towards

the rocks at World's End. The three
mysterious stones seemed to sparkle in
the starlight. Two tall and one round –
the gateway through which Tor and
Mistral would hopefully escape back to
their own world.

But only if I can break the stone,
thought Erin.

Erin saw Chloe's camouflage drop
briefly as she landed in the shadows

between the two tall stones. It was a
good place to hide. They could only
be seen if someone flew directly
above them and looked down. She
joined her and let her own camouflage
drop too.

'Here!' Chloe thrust the trapping
stone into her hands. 'Do the spell!'

Erin felt panic rising inside her. 'But
I don't know what to do. Not really.'

'Just do as Tor told you,' said Chloe.
She looked at her confidently. 'You can
do it, Erin!'

Erin knelt down. What had Tor said
earlier in the woods? *Water made the
trapping stone what it is and water can also
destroy it . . . You must use your stardust
magic to call up rain. You must make the
rain flow through the hole in the centre of*

the trapping stone . . . When the stone splits, I will do the rest.

But how can he when Marianne's got him? she thought.

She shifted position uncomfortably. The shingle was cold and wet beneath her knees. Glancing up at the sky, she saw that Marianne was still taunting Tor, but for how much longer? If she went to the cave, she would quickly realize the stone was missing . . .

Erin put the trapping stone down in her lap and took the seeing stone out of her pocket. She had to start the spell. She had to do her bit and then they could worry about Tor later. Fear clawed at her stomach. But what if she couldn't do it? What if Marianne somehow sensed she was doing this and came into the vision and stopped her?

Erin bit her lip. She felt just as she had that morning when she had been about to get on Kestrel – she was scared.

But I did get on him, she thought. *I was scared, but I did it. I stopped Tango and I rode Kestrel later too.*

Shutting out the noise of the sea and the feel of the shingle under her legs, she stared at the hole in the seeing stone.

I want to break the trapping stone, she thought. *I don't care about Marianne. I just have to do it.*

A wave of blackness swept instantly over her as though it had been waiting for her to make that decision. When the world went dark, all the sounds stopped too. She was suddenly surrounded by a velvety-soft silence, just as she imagined the silence would be at the bottom of a deep, dark well.

The darkness cleared. To her surprise, she realized she was in exactly the same place, kneeling on the spit of land beside the three rocks of World's End with the trapping stone in her lap and the seeing stone in her hands, but there was no noise and no one else there. The sea was flat and still. The sky was a deep black without a single star.

Erin's hands shook. She was in a vision. And this was her chance to break the trapping stone. She remembered what Tor had said, and looked at the skies.

'Rain be with me!' she called loudly.

Overhead a cloud formed and rain started to fall.

Erin looked at the hole in the trapping stone. She had to send water through it. She concentrated on the rain and imagined it streaming down like a jet of water instead of falling as raindrops.

The raindrops moved together in a ball. Magic crackled through Erin's body. She could feel it building, rising through her, gathering in her fingertips. She sent it rushing out of her towards the water ball in the sky. Sparks lit up the ball of water and then it started to fall in a straight line, like water coming out of a tap. Erin grabbed the trapping stone and held it up in her right hand. The stream of water headed down from the skies towards the stone.

A wild shriek shattered the air. 'No!'

CHAPTER

Eleven

Erin jumped in shock. Darkness fell and she cried out in alarm as real life seemed to rush back at her – the noise of the sea, the cold stones under her legs, the water on her skin . . .

She realized that, just as in her vision, there were clouds in the sky and it was raining in real life. Because she had lost her concentration, the rain had formed into drops again. *No*, thought Erin, instinctively focusing on it and forcing it back into a stream. She swept the trapping stone up again to meet the water coming down from the sky. She had to get the stream of water through it and complete the spell!

But I'm not in a vision any more, she thought. *It's not going to work. I'm not powerful enough! Tor said I had to be in a vision!*

But she couldn't give up. She held the stone high.

'Erin!' cried Chloe from behind her. 'Marianne's coming!'

Erin looked round wildly.

Marianne was streaking down from the sky. 'You shall not stop me!' The dark spirit lifted her hands. 'Rain be with me!'

As Marianne's attention was taken up

by Erin, her hold on Tor lessened. He
struck out with his hooves, tearing
through the misty ropes that were
holding him. Marianne didn't notice;
she was too busy turning the rain she
had called up into a jet of water.

'You will not do this!' the dark spirit
hissed. She sent the water she had
conjured straight at Erin's raincloud to
blast it away. But as it collided with the

raincloud there was a flash of searing white light, bright as the brightest lightning, and the cloud exploded! Arrows made of water filled the sky. But they were not made from ordinary water; they sparkled with magic.

Marianne cried out in alarm. 'What's happening?'

There was a whinny and Tor, free from the ropes at last, galloped down from above.

'What's going on, Tor?' gasped Erin as he landed on the shingle.

But before he could answer, several things happened at once. One of the arrows of water shot straight through the hole in the trapping stone Erin was still holding. There was a loud cracking noise and the brown stone broke apart in Erin's hand. Mist started to stream out of it as Erin dropped it in shock.

At the same moment, another arrow of water shot through the hole in the giant round hagstone. It exploded with an enormous bang. Chunks of rock ricocheted through the sky.

'Erin! Watch out!' yelled Chloe as the rocks started to rain down around them. She pulled Erin to one side just in time as a boulder landed where Erin had been standing.

Erin glanced up and saw that the rocks were missing Marianne. She seemed to be surrounded by an invisible barrier of protection.

Erin grabbed her own warding stone from her pocket. 'Protect us!' she gasped. The rocks continued to pelt down, but now they seem to fall around her and Chloe, never coming closer than a metre away. Tor seemed unaffected: any rocks that touched him made no impact on his cloud body. He walked forward, his eyes fixed on the shimmering mist hovering above the broken trapping stone that was lying on the shingle.

'No!' shrieked Marianne, flying towards them.

'Fire be with me!' Chloe shot her hand out. A fireball flew from the tips of her fingers straight at Marianne, sizzling as the raindrops fell on it.

The fireball bounced off the invisible barrier around Marianne created by her own warding stone, but it distracted her, making her look round. Tor galloped straight at her.

Marianne stepped backwards instinctively and stumbled over one of the chunks of rock on the ground. As she did, Erin saw a hagstone fall from her pocket.

'She's dropped her warding stone!'

Tor reared up over the dark spirit, his front legs striking out. They lashed down towards Marianne's head. She cried out and ducked away just in time.

Tor's body seemed to swell and grow, a cloud threatening to engulf the dark spirit. Marianne turned and raced away. Tor plunged after her, mouth open, ears flattened, but suddenly she vanished into thin air. Erin looked around in alarm. She must have camouflaged herself. Where was she?

Tor smelt the air, his eyes alert. He

paused for a few seconds and then with a triumphant toss of his head he swung round and cantered back towards them. 'The dark one has fled,' he said. He landed lightly on the shingle and walked towards the broken trapping stone where the mist was still hovering.

'Is that Mistral?' Chloe breathed.

Tor did not reply. Reaching out with his nose, he touched the mist gently. It seemed to vibrate slightly.

Tor breathed out a soft sound, halfway between a whicker and a word.

The mist shook more strongly. It grew denser and formed a shape, the shape of a miniature grey colt. Suddenly it expanded outwards and a foal was standing there in front of them. His back was level with Erin's shoulder; his eyes had the same proud look as Tor's.

Tor whinnied in delight. 'Mistral!'

The foal reared up and shook back his stubby mane. 'Father!'

'You are free,' said Tor.

Overhead dense clouds started to scud across the sky and rain started to fall.

'Mistral, this is Chloe – and Erin.' Tor's eyes held Erin's for a moment and she saw the gratitude in them. 'They have helped to free you.'

'Thank you,' whickered Mistral.

'I don't know quite how we did it,' said Erin wonderingly. 'I thought you said I had to be in a vision for the magic, Tor.'

'It would have been true,' Tor replied. 'But when the stream of water you were calling down from the skies met the water Marianne was conjuring there was a magical explosion and a release of power great enough to split not just the trapping stone but also the gateway.'

'Why was there so much power?' Chloe asked, looking at the destroyed gateway.

Tor looked at Erin. 'I am not exactly sure. But there is one possible explanation. Do you remember what I told you about family links being very important in weather weaving?'

Erin nodded. 'Yes, you said it was better to use my mum's hagstones because my magic would add to her magic.'

Tor nodded. 'That is because there is a link between the magic of weather weavers who are related, the power from one adds to the power of the other. I believe that is what happened just now.'

Erin frowned. That didn't make sense. 'But I'm not related to Marianne.'

Tor breathed out. 'I think you may be.'

There was silence for a moment. Erin stared at him.

'Oh,' Chloe whispered. She gazed at Erin, as if seeing her with new eyes. 'I suppose you do look a bit like her.'

'No!'

exclaimed Erin, shaking her head. 'I can't be related to Marianne! I'd know if I was!' Tor had got it wrong. 'I just can't be.' She went on. 'My mum was an only child and my gran was too. I haven't got any aunts or cousins or anything like that.'

Tor looked at her gently. 'I do not understand how it can be. I just know that is the only possible reason why there might have been such an explosion of power when your magic met.'

Chloe squeezed Erin's hand. 'Maybe there is some other explanation though.'

'There has to be!' insisted Erin.

'Look, forget it for now. What's important is getting Tor and Mistral back to the sky,' said Chloe, looking at the sky horses. 'How are we going to do that now the gateway is broken?'

'We must find another gateway,' Tor said.

'What about the one under water?' said Chloe. 'That Marianne was making.'

'It's raining now,' Erin pointed out. 'That's stopped there being six days of clear sky.'

Chloe looked at Tor. 'So? Couldn't you and Erin work together to make another six days of calm so it formed in the water again?'

'Unfortunately, Erin would need to be with me every hour of the day and night,' Tor said. 'Her magic is not as strong as Marianne's and the effect of sending me into the sky would not last. I would need to be there all the time for six days to keep the clouds away.'

'Oh,' said Chloe slowly. 'We can't do that then. Jo and your dad would want to know where you were, Erin. So what are we going to do?'

'We must find another gateway,' Tor said. 'If there is one.'

A memory was pulling at Erin's mind. She realized what it was and took a piece of paper out of her pocket. 'There is! I'm sure. I found this in the cave. Do you remember the prophecy that Marianne spoke the night Mistral came through the giant hagstone? Well, this is the same prophecy and it talks about gateways. Listen.' She read out the first six lines:

'When the dark one returns, the door
   shall be reopened

And danger will threaten all living below.
If the binding is broken, they can be
    protected,
But one coming willingly lets the dark's
    power grow
Until the first gateway is split by magic
And he who is trapped is free to go.'

Erin broke off. 'That bit's come true
already.'

Chloe nodded. 'The gateway has just
been split by magic, and Mistral has
been freed.'

'Is there more to the prophecy?' Tor
asked eagerly.

'Yes,' Erin told him. 'It says: *Two*
gateways now balance the light and the
darkness, one lost in memory, hidden by the
sea.'

'Two more gateways,' said Tor, his eyes suddenly looking very interested. 'The dark door we cannot use, but this prophecy makes it sound as if there is another gateway as well. One lost in memory.'

'And it seems to have some clues in it as to where it might be,' said Erin, holding up the paper eagerly. 'Oh, Tor. I bet we can find it!'

'We won't stop until we do!' said Chloe. 'And then you and Mistral will be able to go back to the clouds.'

Mistral butted his head affectionately against Chloe, and Tor nuzzled him. 'We will get back,' he told his son. 'We will find the lost gateway and return to our kingdom.'

Erin's thoughts raced. So much had happened that night. The giant hagstone had been destroyed, but at least Mistral was free and another gateway was waiting somewhere. *But so is Marianne*, she thought as an image of the dark spirit filled her head – Marianne, as she had been the time she had tempted Erin to cross through the vision, her lips curving into a familiar smile.

My smile, Erin realized with a jolt.

She felt Tor's breath on her shoulder and the image of Marianne faded. Erin lifted her chin. Right then, she wouldn't let thoughts of the dark weather weaver upset her any more. The most important thing was getting Mistral and Tor back to the clouds.

We'll find the lost gateway, she thought, her fingers curling round the hair that was still caught in her watchstrap. *Marianne won't stop us. We're going to set Tor and Mistral free!*

It all started with a Scarecrow

Puffin is well over sixty years old.
Sounds ancient, doesn't it? But Puffin has never been
so lively. We're always on the lookout for the next big
idea, which is how it began all those years ago.

Penguin Books was a big idea from the mind of
a man called Allen Lane, who in 1935 invented
the quality paperback and changed the world.
**And from great Penguins, great Puffins grew,
changing the face of children's books forever.**

The first four Puffin Picture Books were hatched in 1940 and the
first Puffin story book featured a man with broomstick arms called
Worzel Gummidge. In 1967 Kaye Webb, Puffin Editor, started the
Puffin Club, promising to **'make children into readers'**.
She kept that promise and over 200,000 children became
devoted Puffineers through their quarterly installments of
Puffin Post, which is now back for a new generation.

Many years from now, we hope you'll look back and
remember Puffin with a smile. **No matter what your age
or what you're into, there's a Puffin for everyone.**
The possibilities are endless, but one thing is for sure:
whether it's a picture book or a paperback, a sticker book
or a hardback, **if it's got that little Puffin
on it – it's bound to be good.**